P9-DVD-154

Jan. 21, 1987

To:

Tiffany Ross

Your special friends

Mr. Jelly Bean

and

Mr. G.

Love from your Nana

This is a special friend

I love you !!

# *MR. JELLY BEAN*

By

Ed D. Garehime

Illustrated by

Marianne E. Garehime

Published by

The Deem Corporation
P.O. Box 14
Denver, Colorado 80201

Printed By Tewell's Printing
Denver, Colorado
U.S.A.

 Inquiries should be addressed to: "The Deem Corporation," P.O. Box #14, Denver, Colorado 80201

Second Edition - 1979
Library of Congress Catalog Card No. 77-82261
ISBN 0-918822-01-7

## DEDICATED TO

My wife, Elizabeth, and our daughters, Marianne, Katherine, and Janet. "Thanks for all your help."

## TABLE OF CONTENTS



## PREFACE

If this book is read by or read to a child, that child's name is to be inserted into the blank spaces as they appear in the "Mr. Jelly Bean" stories. The child's name may be written into these spaces, or merely read into the story as the spaces occur. Choose the appropriate pronouns as they appear in the text.

*The Secret Hiding Place*

# Mr. Jelly Bean Meets

........................

[Note: Remember to read your name or the listener's name into the blank spaces.]

Have you ever thought, "I'd surely like to meet someone who was really exciting and super fun to be with, maybe someone from another planet—from outer space?"

Well, wow! Let me tell you what happened to .................! One time not long ago, ................. discovered a secret place to play where the trees were thick and shadowy, where the grass and bushes and flowers and rocks were scattered everywhere between the big trees.

It was a great place to hide—almost like being in another world. .................had taken some of the best rocks and made a pretend throne next to a large tree. Sometimes when sitting there, ................. would close her/his eyes and just listen to all of the sounds—like the wind softly blowing through the trees and the little birds chirping.

Late one afternoon the strangest thing happened! While sitting on the throne , . . . . . . . . . . . . . . . . thought that she/he heard a small voice calling. Sitting up quickly to listen and see better, . . . . . . . . . . . . . . . . distinctly heard, ". . . . . . . . . . . . . . . . , . . . . . . . . . . . . . . . . , is that you?"

*Did Someone Call Me?*

*Where Are You?*

"I, I, I'm over here," . . . . . . . . . . . . . . . . was finally able to say,"but where are you?"

"I'm right here," the faint little voice said.

After looking as far as possible through the trees and not seeing anyone, . . . . . . . . . . . . . . . . called loudly, "Where are you?"

"You don't have to shout," the little voice answered, "I'm down here by your feet standing next to this big red flower."

.................looked down and couldn't believe what she/he saw. All that could be seen looking up between the leaves was a small face with the cutest smile and the biggest and brightest eyes.

*Such A Cute Smile And The Brightest Eyes*

"Who, who are you? You're so small! Are you a real person? Where did you come from? How did you know my name?" ................ asked in rapid succession.

"Whoa, now," the little fellow said, "not so many questions. First of all, I want to be your friend. Let me introduce myself. I am Mr. Xanthozenthum. My home is on the planet Therma in the Andromeda star constellation which is in the Northern Celestial Hemisphere. You are so much larger than me; I hope that you won't want to hurt me, because you could step on me and flatten me out like a pancake."

*Mr. Jelly Bean*

"Oh, I wouldn't do that, Mr. Xantho—something," .................interrupted; "I'm sorry that I can't pronounce your name and I don't know where you live, but you're certainly a little person. I wouldn't hurt you either because—because you're so cute. Why, you look almost, well, almost like a jelly bean."

Oh, golly! Not many of us would like to be called a jelly bean; but Mr. Xanthozenthum was super-nice and said, "If you can't pronounce my name, why don't you call me what I look like—Mr. Jelly Bean?"

"Mr. Jelly Bean! Neat-o!" ................. replied while kneeling down to get a better look at him. "Mr. Jelly Bean! I'd like to call you Mr. Jelly Bean! But what are you doing here in my secret hiding place?"

Now that Mr. Jelly Bean was quite certain that ................ would not harm him, he stepped out from under the flowers, put his hands on his hips, and said in a stern voice, "It will take me time to answer all of your questions."

*It Will Take Me Time To Answer All Of Your Questions*

"But first," Mr. Jelly Bean continued, "I want you to stand up and hold one of your hands out in front of you, palm up —good—Hold your hand still now."

Before ................. realized what had happened, Mr. Jelly Bean jumped from the ground right into her/his outstretched hand. As anyone would do, she/he pulled her/his hand back so fast that Mr. Jelly Bean would have fallen "kersplat" back on the ground if he hadn't grabbed onto ...............'s little finger and hung on for dear life with his little legs kicking in the air.

*Help!*

While ................. was trying to figure out the best way to help him, two antennae that were protruding from the top of Mr. Jelly Bean's head began to sparkle. As ................. watched, Mr. Jelly Bean floated around her/his hand and then gently landed back on top. With that ................. breathed nervously, "Mr. Jelly Bean, how did you do that?"

"I'm sorry if I startled you again," he apologized. "I suppose that I should tell you about my antennae which you might think are magical."

*I Have Magical Antennae*

"On my planet we all have two antennae with which we can do almost anything we choose. My antennae told me your language and your name. I can use them to do many things, like move those rocks by that big tree."

"Oh, please don't do that! Those rocks are my pretend throne," ................ quickly replied.

"Well, that's a nice throne," Mr. Jelly Bean commented, "but wouldn't you like a better one?"

As he paused just a moment, still standing in ................'s hand, his antennae began to sparkle again. He nodded them toward the throne. Instantly the rocks disappeared; and in their place was the most beautiful solid gold throne that you ever saw!

"Mr. Jelly Bean! I can't believe it; I just can't believe it!" .................shrieked almost dropping him again. She/He didn't realize that Mr. Jelly Bean was again kicking madly in the air while hanging on to her/his little finger.

"Oh, sugar!" Mr. Jelly Bean exclaimed quite loudly. "It's obvious that your hand isn't the safest place to stand. I'll just float out in the air in front of you, O.K.?"

Mr. Jelly Bean floating in the air! This was too much! ................. just stared at him hardly able to move or speak.

Finally,................. said slowly but emphatically, "I don't know how you can float out there in the air; but one thing for sure, we'll have to get rid of the gold throne. We definitely must!"

*A Solid-Gold Throne!*

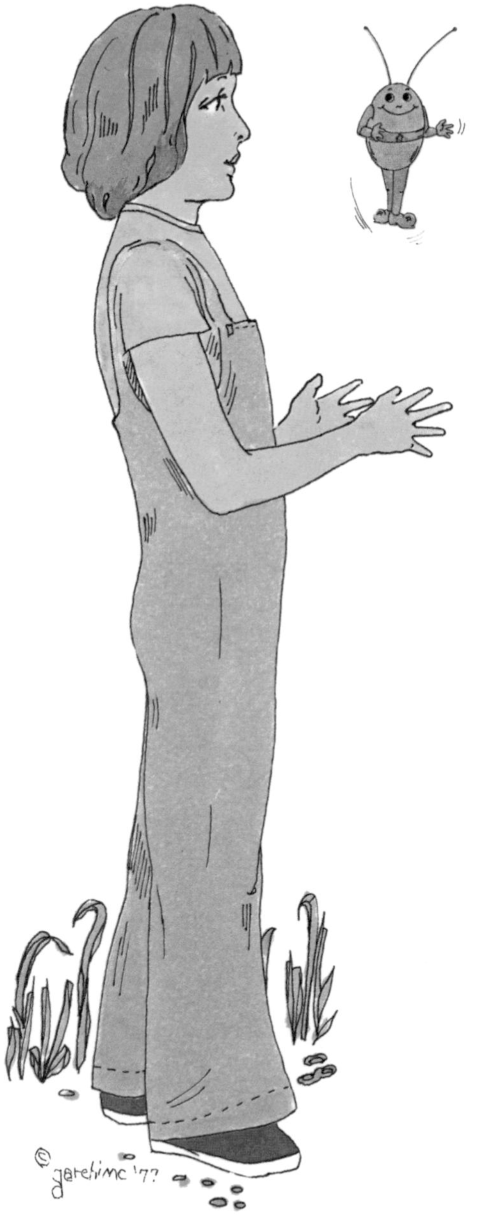

"Don't you like it?" the surprised Mr. Jelly Bean asked, as he floated back and forth and around the gold throne. "Golly, if you want, I'll put some diamonds and rubies around the top, silver angels on either side, and....."

....."Stop, stop, stop! Mr. Jelly Bean," exclaimed .................. "You're a very kind person, I'm sure; and I don't want to hurt your feelings, but the throne is too valuable—it's too much! There are people here on earth who are very, very bad and evil. They would steal all the diamonds and take away all the gold."

*Mr. Jelly Bean is Very Kind*

"Oh, sugar, I was hoping that everyone on earth was as good as you are," Mr. Jelly Bean said somewhat disappointedly. "Yes, ................., I can understand why there shouldn't be a solid gold throne. I'll change it back to the way it was."

He then nodded his sparkling antennae toward the throne and "zingo"—it was stone again.

................. politely said, "Thank you, Mr. Jelly Bean. A gold throne would have caused lots of trouble."

Then Mr. Jelly Bean asked, "Did you know that you're my first earth friend? If you would like to, we can do lots of wonderful things together. Would you like to fly around in the air just like I'm doing now?"

*Oh Sugar!*

"Oh, golly, yes!" ................. quickly replied, "I mean, no! I mean, yes! Oh, I don't know! Would I fall? Is it scary? Oh, gosh, Mr. Jelly Bean, could I really fly all by myself?"

*Yipes, An Ant Larger Than A Cat!*

"Not a thing to worry about," Mr. Jelly Bean said reassuringly, "There's a requirement though; you must be small like me."

"How can I become your size?" ................asked very surprised.

"First, close your eyes," Mr. Jelly Bean said, talking more like an instructor now, "and stand very still." ................ obeyed almost instinctively. Then, as Mr. Jelly Bean nodded his sparkling antennae, ................ felt a slight tingling sensation; and on the command, "Open your eyes," ................ saw that she/he was almost as small as Mr. Jelly Bean—the flowers appeared as big as trees, an ant looked larger than a cat! And, yipes! the sight of a big black bug sent ................ running over to Mr. Jelly Bean for protection.

*Flowers Large As Trees*

"Everthing is so huge! I'm scared, Mr. Jelly Bean!"

"Oh, sugar! You don't have a thing to worry about," he said reassuringly. "If you'll just listen, Mr. Black Bug is trying to say 'hello' to you."

As ................ hung more tightly than ever onto Mr. Jelly Bean, the best reply that she/he could make was a squeaky, "Oh, hello, Mr. Bug."

"This may be another surprise to you ................, but you don't have to be afraid anymore," Mr. Jelly Bean calmly said, "and do you know why? Well, it's because you now have two small antennae like mine. With them you can protect yourself; you can talk to anyone; you can fly; you can do almost anything."

Gosh, what would you do if someone said that you had two antennae sticking up from the top of your head? I'll bet that you would reach up to feel if they were really there. That's exactly what ................ did; and sure enough, the antennae were there!

................ wiggled the antennae back and forth and pulled on them a little—they were really stuck on tightly. So that ................ would be comfortable with her/his new antennae, Mr. Jelly Bean explained carefully how to use them, how to protect them, and even how to keep them clean.

*I Really Do Have Two Antennae*

Well, after ................. got her/his courage back, she/he and Mr. Jelly Bean had a super good talk with Mr. Black Bug and Mrs. Red Ant.

With all the exciting and marvelous things happening, ................. forgot about home and what time it was. When Mrs. Red Ant said that she had to leave to gather more food for supper, ................. then remembered that she/he had to hurry home to have supper, too.

"Golly, Mr. Black Bug and Mrs. Red Ant," ................. said, "I'm certainly glad that we are friends. Maybe sometime you could come over to my house, O.K.? I've got to go home now; so bye, bye, and I hope to see you soon."

*Bye, Bye, See You Soon*

When ................. turned to leave, she/he tripped—"kerplunk"—over a big old weed.

*A Tumble Into The Weeds*

Maybe it wasn't the most polite thing to do, but Mr. Jelly Bean, Mr. Black Bug, and Mrs. Red Ant had a good laugh when all that they could see was .................'s legs sticking out above the weeds.

Then almost at the same time they all called out, "Are you hurt? Can we help you?"

"Oh, thank you for wanting to help me, but I'm O.K.," ................. exclaimed, as she/he quickly stood up and brushed the dust from her/his clothes. "I forgot that I was still small."

After all said "good-byes" again, Mr. Black Bug and Mrs. Red Ant disappeared down the path that led around the big red flowers.

Then ................. turned to Mr. Jelly Bean and asked, "I'm so small; how will I ever get home?"

"................," Mr. Jelly Bean answered, "You forgot that with our antennae we can do nearly anything that we want to. We'll fly home! Then I'll make you big again. All that you have to do is think about flying and away you'll go."

"Gosh," ................ said, "If you think that I can fly, I'll surely try."

Mr. Jelly Bean took ................ by the hand and said, "O.K., now we'll practice flying only a little way off the ground."

................ was amazed how easy it was—just floating around a few meters above the ground. Then they flew higher and higher; and before long they were sailing over the tallest tree tops.

*It's Easy To Fly*

*Flying Faster and Faster—What Fun!*

You may not believe this; but ................ was not at all afraid, and quickly learned to fly like a bird.

Let me tell you what that little rascal, ................, did! Before Mr. Jelly Bean realized what was happening, ................ started to fly faster and faster; soon all of the birds around were chasing after her/him. Then, of all things, ................ started to dive and spin and loop-the-loop and do all kinds of wild flying.

The surprised Mr. Jelly Bean flew after her/him and warned, "Be careful, you could kill yourself!" But ................ kept right on flying as wildly as ever—up, down, and all around, scattering the little birds every which way. Two big old hawks were nearly "clobbered."

Finally, in desperation, Mr. Jelly Bean called out, “I thought that you had to go right home for supper.” When ................ heard that, you never saw anyone stop so fast!

“Oh, my gosh,” ................ exclaimed, “Daddy will be home for dinner soon. I must go! But I apologize, Mr. Jelly Bean, I didn’t know that flying could be so much fun, wow!”

“I can understand your excitement,” Mr. Jelly Bean replied, “but you nearly took a wing off Mr. Hawk. If you would have been listening, as you should have, you would have heard how Mr. Hawk was scolding you. He was really angry. So be careful in the future, O.K.?”

*Mr. Hawk Was Nearly Clobbered.*

After ................. assured him that it would never happen again, Mr. Jelly Bean took her/him by the hand and quickly led the way back home where they landed near the entry steps.

*How Am I Going To Get Up This Step?*

Because ................. was still small, the steps looked almost like a mountain. When she/he tried to reach up to climb over the first step, Mr. Jelly Bean said, "Wait a moment, I must make you big again. If your father came walking down the steps and didn't see you, can you imagine what might happen to you? When you're small, you have to be extra careful."

Mr. Jelly Bean continued, "I'll make you big now; so just close your eyes again."

"Ka-zippo," ................. was full size again. And not any too soon, because just then, Mother opened the door and called, ". . . . . . . . . . . . . . . . . come to dinner."

"I'll be right in," ............... answered, "but first I'd like to say good-bye to a new friend of mine."

*Good-bye, Mr. Jelly Bean*

................ hurriedly told Mr. Jelly Bean, who had been hiding back of the entry steps, that she/he would meet him the next day at their secret hiding place. Mr. Jelly Bean agreed to the plan; and suggested that they might go for a ride in his rocket ship, maybe to the moon. .............. was so excited about flying with Mr. Jelly Bean the next day that she/he almost forgot to wave good-bye to him as he disappeared over the tree tops to return to his rocket ship.

*Good-bye, See You Tomorrow*

During dinner when Mother asked ................. who the new friend was, she/he answered, "Oh, it's Mr. Jelly Bean. He's from outer space. We flew around with all kinds of birds today, and tomorrow we may fly to the moon in his rocket ship. I really want you and Daddy to meet him. He's super nice."

Daddy winked at Mother and then said, "You always had a great imagination; but if you bring Mr. Jelly Bean home sometime, we'd be very happy to meet him."

Actually, Daddy and Mother didn't believe that there was a Mr. Jelly Bean; but just between you and me, we know that Mr. Jelly Bean is a wonderful little fellow who came from the planet Therma; and, for sure, we know that he picked . . . . . . . . . . . . . . . . . to be his extra special friend.

*Oh, I Really Wish That You Could Meet*

*My Friend, Mr. Jelly Bean!*

## *THE CONSTELLATION ANDROMEDA*

Mr. Jelly Bean in our stories is a mythical person; but there really is the Constellation Andromeda in the Northern Celestial Hemisphere. During the months of November and December in the U.S.A., the constellation can be seen in the southern skies. A "Star Chart" is useful for identifying the constellations. Among the farthest lights in the sky visible to the unaided eye is the Great Spiral Galaxy in Andromeda. It is approximately two million (2,000,000) light years away.

Other than our sun, our nearest star is in the constellation Centaurus; it is called "Proxima Centauri" and is over four light years away. If we could travel to "Proxima Centauri" in one of our rocket ships at 40,000 kilometers (approximately 25,000 miles) an hour (which is about as fast as man has traveled), the trip there would take over one hundred and fourteen thousand (114,000) years.

NOTE: A light-year is the distance that light travels in one year moving at approximately 300,000 kilometers (186,282 miles) each second.

# MR. JELLY BEAN AND ..............................
# MEET THE BAD MR. HAS BEAN

## (When They Visit The Moon)

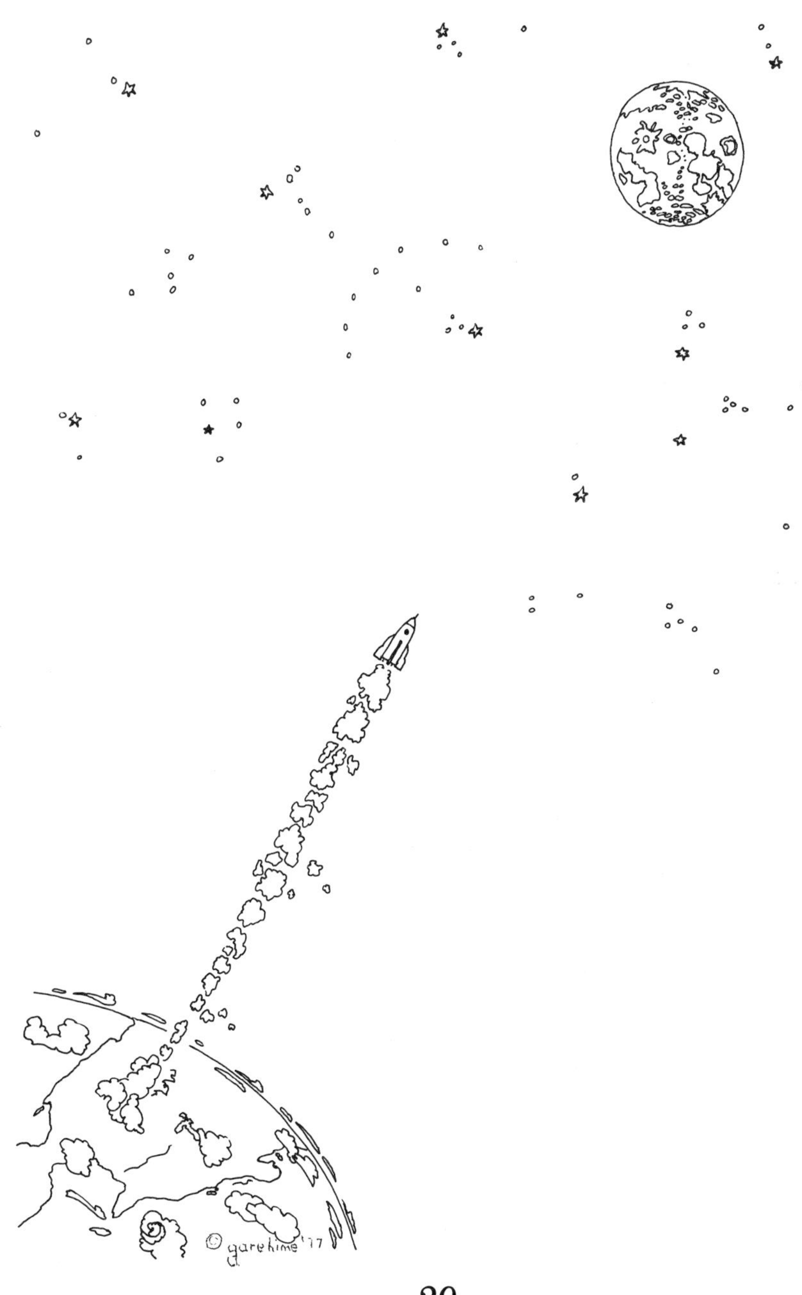

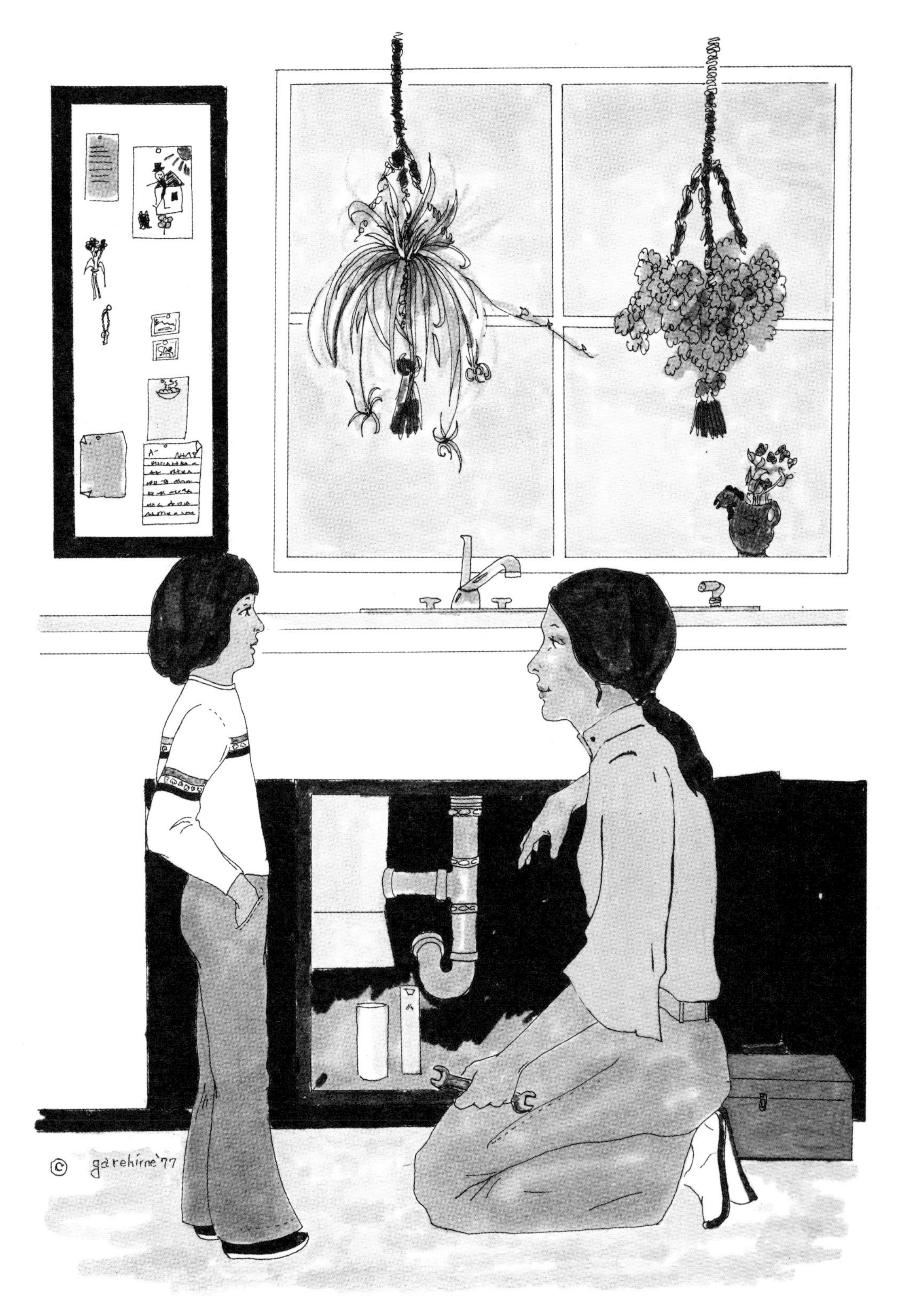
© garehime'77

# *Mr. Jelly Bean and .................................... Meet the Bad Mr. Has Bean*

Mr. Jelly Bean, as most of us know, came from the far-away planet called "Therma." He is a wonderful little fellow with two antennae that seem almost magical; because with them he can do so many marvelous things. Mr. Jelly Bean is so much fun to be with!

Very soon after ................. and Mr. Jelly Bean met for the first time, they became the best of friends; so when Mr. Jelly Bean offered ................. a ride in his rocket ship, she/he didn't hesitate to ask, "May we go right now?"

"Well, not right now," Mr. Jelly Bean replied, "How about tomorrow afternoon? Get permission from your folks first, and then meet me at your secret hiding place around noon time."

You can be sure that ................. could hardly wait for the next day to arrive—a ride in a real rocket ship—wow!

At noon the next day what do you think ................. asked her/his mother? You are right! She/He asked if she/he could go for a ride in Mr. Jelly Bean's rocket ship and, maybe, fly all the way to the moon and back.

Mother's answer seemed rather casual when she said, "O.K., but don't fly too fast."

Well now, with such a reply it might seem that Mother didn't care if ................ went to the moon or not; but actually Mother didn't think that there really was a Mr. Jelly Bean with a rocket ship. She thought that ................ was just playing make-believe, as she/he had done many times before.

However, as ................ hurried out of the house she/he assured her/his mother that Mr. Jelly Bean was a very careful pilot and that they'd be back before dinner.

Even though ................ arrived early at the secret hiding place, Mr. Jelly Bean was already there, calmly sitting just inside the open hatch of his rocket ship.

"Hi, Mr. Jelly Bean," ................ said somewhat out of breath, "Are we going for a ride now?"

"All checked out and programmed for a flight to the moon. Just walk up these steps and come on in through the hatch. But don't bump your head; it's a little low."

"Mr. Jelly Bean! I can't. I'm too big!" ................ quickly replied.

"Oh, sugar! I forgot to make you small again," Mr. Jelly Bean said softly.

Before ................. could say another word, Mr. Jelly Bean's antennae began to sparkle and "zip, zing," she/he was small again.

*Hello There!*

"Oh, thank you, Mr. Jelly Bean. I'm not used to being small; because, golly, everything else all of a sudden becomes so big—the flowers are like trees, wow! And, and—oh, look over there! Here comes Mrs. Red Ant and Mr. Black Bug again."

"Hello there," ................. shouted, "Are you coming with us to the moon?"

Because ................. now had two magical antennae like Mr. Jelly Bean's, she/he could easily understand Mr. Black Bug as he replied, "Mr. Jelly Bean asked Mrs. Red Ant and me if we wanted to go along, but we have to gather sugar berries that must be stored for food for this coming winter. We would like to go next time, if we may. We'll wait to wave good-bye. Have a nice trip."

By this time Mr. Jelly Bean was standing on the ground beside the rocket ship so that he could help ................. up the steps. ................. had never seen the inside of a real rocket ship; so she/he hurried over to Mr. Jelly Bean who took her/him by the hand and led the way up the steps and into the control room.

"Oh, neato," .................exclaimed, "all those buttons, and dials and things. What happens if you pull that shiny lever?"

"Don't get too excited now," Mr. Jelly Bean quickly answered, "and don't touch anything until I teach you all about the controls, O.K.?"

"Do you really think that I could learn to fly this rocket ship?" ................. continued, "What does this red button do? This green one? This blue one? What do those squiggly lines on that TV picture mean?"

"Be patient, I'll tell you all about the buttons, and dials, and other controls as we fly along to the moon," Mr. Jelly Bean said, as he settled himself into the pilot-in-command seat. "You sit in the co-pilot's seat next to me on my right."

*I'll Help You Up The Steps*

*This Is The Control Room*

................. carefully climbed into the large, padded seat; then, following Mr. Jelly Bean's instructions, fastened the seat belt, adjusted the head rest, and moved a little lever that tilted the seat back to the blast-off position.

The quiet rocket ship suddenly seemed to come alive. All kinds of things started to happen! Mr. Jelly Bean was quickly pushing buttons, pulling levers, and turning knobs, as he loudly read through a pre-lift-off check list.

"Close hatch door"..... Bang!

"Pressurize cabin"..... Sssssssssssss!

"Start giros"..... Whrrrrrrrrr!

"Adjust rocket fuel mixture"..... Ffffffffff!

"Forward and rear TV pictures on"..... Click! Click!

................. listened intently as Mr. Jelly Bean continued the check-out. Finally, Mr. Jelly Bean paused and said loudly, "Ignite engines .... We have lift-off!"

Can you imagine how excited ................. was as she/he heard the rumble of the powerful rocket engines and felt the G-forces push her/his body back into the padded seat, as they headed straight up into the sky?

In the rear TV picture ................. saw Mrs. Red Ant and Mr. Black Bug waving good-bye; and, as their speed increased rapidly, the earth seemed to move away at a frightening rate.

As the G-forces on .................'s body became less and less and she/he could lift both hands from the arm rests, she/he became aware that Mr. Jelly Bean was counting, "Mach 198, Mach 199, now holding at Mach 200, inertial guidance on automatic sequence for flight, deceleration and landing. We are traveling almost 225,000 kilometers (140,000 miles) per hour. Now we can unfasten our seat belts and relax for a while, O.K.?"

*Waving Good-Bye*

"I hear you, Mr. Jelly Bean. Wow! What a lift-off. Look how small
the earth is and how much larger the moon is getting!"
© garehime' 77

With zero gravity and the seat belts unfastened, ................. started to float away from her/his seat and then began shouting loudly, "Help, help! Hold me down!"

"Now settle down and quit kicking around so," Mr. Jelly Bean said in a calm but stern voice. "We'll have zero gravity for about an hour. So that you can easily walk around, I'll put these magnetic shoes on your feet..... hold still..... there's one..... there's the other. Now you have both magnets securely on your feet. It's O.K. to walk in those areas marked with the big green dots. I'll show you how to walk correctly by turning the magnets off and on."

*Help! Hold Me Down!*

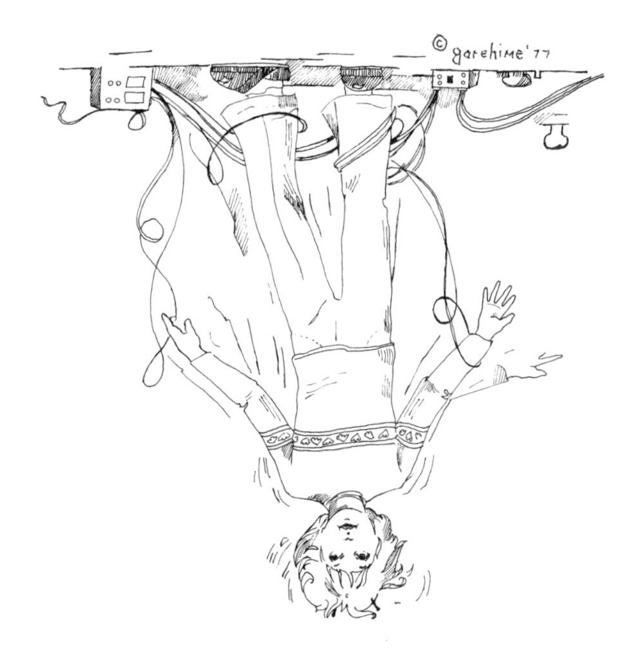

## *You're Getting All Tangled Up*

Mr. Jelly Bean continued, "First, you have to — ................. what are you doing up there on the ceiling? And be careful! You're getting all tangled up in the wires!"

"Oh, Mr. Jelly Bean," ................. tried to explain, "All I did was try to push hard to get my feet loose from the floor, when all of a sudden I went flying up here!"

It's a good thing that Mr. Jelly Bean had lots of patience and didn't get angry very easily, because it took some time to untangle ................. and then teach her/him the correct walking procedure.

Before very long, ................. was walking so well that Mr. Jelly Bean had her/him come over to the main control panel to begin her/his first flight lesson.

You would think that with so many buttons, knobs, and levers, that it would be very difficult to learn what they were all for; but ................. learned very, very rapidly. The two antennae that Mr. Jelly Bean had given her/him made ................. super, super smart! So it didn't take long for her/him to learn how to fly almost as well as Mr. Jelly Bean.

Fifteen minutes prior to moon-orbit insertion, the landing sequence had to be established.

Mr. Jelly Bean called out in a commanding voice, "For the landing on the moon, we must return to our seats, fasten safety belts, and prepare for rocket rotation, deceleration, and touch down."

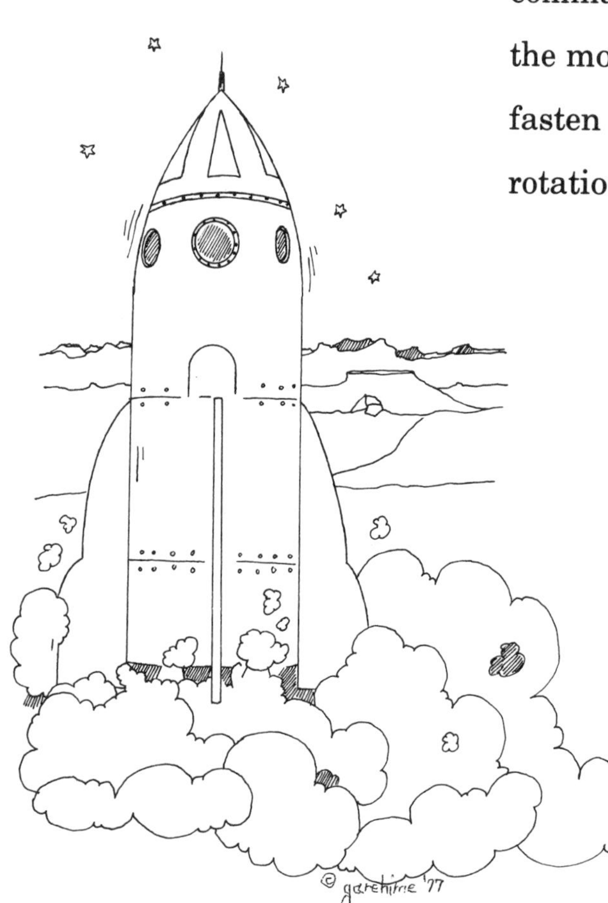

*Landing On The Moon*

After again securely fastening her/his seat belt, ................. listened carefully as Mr. Jelly Bean read through the landing procedure.

Soon the rocky surface of the moon appeared on the TV screen; and before very long, a solid thump was felt..... they had landed on the moon!

"Open the hatch, Mr. Jelly Bean," ................ said the moment they were out of their seats. Before Mr. Jelly Bean could answer, ................ continued, "I know that the moon doesn't have much gravity to hold me down; so I want to run around out there and see how far and high I can jump..... jumpity jump, jump..... let's go, go, go!"

"Great stars above," Mr. Jelly Bean exclaimed. "In outer space you must stop to think before you do anything. Do you want to kill yourself? Because there is no air on the moon and, therefore, no air pressure, if I'd open the hatch door right now, we'd blow up all over the place."

"We must first put on our space suits. Because we both have antennae, our space suits won't be like those worn by ordinary people. With our antennae we can create an invisible neutron force-field all around our bodies; and this will protect us from the radiation and the vacuum of space and provide the oxygen that we need to breath."

"Well, Mr. Jelly Bean," ................ replied, "I don't exactly understand all that; but if you say it works, I'm willing to do as you tell me."

Mr. Jelly Bean continued, "Do exactly as I tell you and you'll be O.K."

"First take off the magnetic shoes, because the moon does have a little gravity...... Good! Now stand in front of me..... not too close! Start whirling both of your antennae around in the same direction..... that's excellent! I'll bet that you didn't know that you could do that! Whirl your antennae faster and faster until you can feel something like electrical energy leaving their tips."

Mr. Jelly Bean continued the instructions, "Here comes the amazing part—think very hard about that energy and cause it to flow around your body. Think very hard ..... harder ..... still harder! It's moving! It's moving! It's moving down over your shoulders! You're doing it! Keep it up! You're terrific! I didn't know that you could learn so fast. Now close the force field under and around your feet..... you've done it! You will notice that the completed force-field can not be seen; it's invisible, but it's there." You're safe now to leave the space ship."

*Forming The Force-Field*

Because ................. was listening so carefully to Mr. Jelly Bean's instructions and thinking so hard, she/he wasn't able to say one word. But now that the force-field was completed, ................. was finally able to say rather weakly, "Golly, I didn't know that I could do that."

Mr. Jelly Bean formed the force-field around his own body very quickly. He then moved over to the hatch, turned two unlocking levers, and swung the door open.

*Soon The Hatch Door Was Open*

"We have landed just north of the Carpathian Mountains near a narrow, deep canyon," Mr. Jelly Bean continued, "Come over here by the open hatch door. See, there's the rocky surface of the moon! Over there is the deep canyon that I want to show you. Because your antennae are now strong enough, you can use them to fly anywhere that you want to go."

*Flying Off Across The Moon*

"We will not have to use the steps to leave the ship," Mr. Jelly Bean said.

Whenever ................ was with Mr. Jelly Bean, she/he was not afraid to try anything; so it was "easy-as-pie" to jump from the open hatch of the rocket ship and go flying off across the moon.

Mr. Jelly Bean flew ahead of ................ and led the way over to the narrow canyon. They flew along the canyon rim for perhaps two kilometers when Mr. Jelly Bean said, "Here we will fly down into the canyon and land on that yellow ledge near the bottom."

You should have seen how well ................ was flying! She/He made a perfect landing right beside Mr. Jelly Bean!

The first thing that ................ noticed was that the entire canyon was so very bright and shiny and sparkly.

*A Perfect Landing*

"It's so beautiful down here," ................. said excitedly, "It's like being in a fairy land. The walls look like gold and some of the big rocks look like diamonds!"

"They are," Mr. Jelly Bean said in a matter-of-fact way, "This ledge that we are standing on is solid gold."

Well, all of this so utterly amazed ................. that she/he had to sit down on the nearest big rock to rest for a few minutes. She/He didn't realize it at first, but the rock that she/he was sitting on was really a big diamond!

*Sitting On A Big Diamond*

*Mr. Jelly Bean Made Cosmic Absorption Studies*

Finally, . . . . . . . . . . . . . . . . . became aware that Mr. Jelly Bean was asking her/him if she/he would like to explore the canyon.

"Oh, yes, I'd like very much to go exploring," she/he answered excitedly.

"O.K., we'll use our antennae to fly a few meters above the bottom of the canyon," Mr. Jelly Bean instructed, "Just follow me."

As they slowly flew along, zig-zagging around the large boulders of solid gold and diamonds, Mr. Jelly Bean told how he had discovered the canyon when he was making cosmic absorption studies of our solar system. He told how the canyon was formed millions of years ago and what might happen to it in the future. One thing that he hoped for was that no bad, greedy person from earth would ever find the canyon with all of its gold and diamonds.

They were about half way through the canyon when Mr. Jelly Bean caught ................. by the arm and stopped very quickly.

"Sh, sh," Mr. Jelly Bean said very quietly. "My antennae tell me that there's someone just around those big rocks up ahead. You stay here and I'll go on alone. But don't make a sound."

When Mr. Jelly Bean started to fly on to see who was there, ................. felt more than a little frightened, and became really concerned when she/he noticed for the first time that Mr. Jelly Bean's antennae were emitting big sparks and moving around in a very threatening way.

*Sh, Sh, Someone Is Up Ahead Of Us*

*The Bad Mr. Ikythornum*

*Mr. Jelly Bean and Mr. Ikythornum Just Before The Fight*

Shortly after Mr. Jelly Bean disappeared around the large rocks, ................. heard him shout, "Mr. Ikythornum, you evil, bad person! What are you doing here?"

A voice was heard to snarl, "Well, if it isn't my old enemy, Mr. Xanthozenthum!" (That was Mr. Jelly Bean's real name when he lived on the planet Therma.) Mr. Ikythornum continued, "What are you doing here?"

Mr. Jelly Bean quickly cut in, "How did you escape from the patrol on the planet Therma? And you don't have to tell me what you're doing here. I can see; you are stealing the gold and diamonds..... you galactic space rat!"

"My antennae work as well as yours," the bad Mr. Ikythornum continued. "They tell me that on earth you're called Mr. Jelly Bean. Ha! What a laugh!"

Mr. Jelly Bean snapped back, "I'm proud to be called Mr. Jelly Bean. Before I'm through with you, you'll be called a—a—a 'Has Bean!' In fact, I'm going to call you that from now on—you—you— Mr. Has Bean!"

"Ha! And I'll call you what I think you are—you, Mr. Jelly Bean," Mr. Has Bean was quick to sneer back.

By this time .................'s curiosity was too great; she/he cautiously looked around the big rock to see who was there.

*Oh, Golly! What Is Going To Happen?*

*The Fight Has Started*

There stood a little man about the same size as Mr. Jelly Bean, except that he was dressed differently and looked really mean. ................. continued to watch as the argument grew louder and louder.

Because Mr. Jelly Bean's and Mr. Has Bean's protective force fields neutralized each other, they were now standing face to face with both of their antennae waving around and almost touching. Their antennae were sparking so intensely that they made a very audible hissing sound.

All of a sudden, the tips of Mr. Jelly Bean's antennae touched the bottom of Mr. Has Bean's antennae. Through the bright flash, ................. could see that Mr. Has Bean was thrown backwards across the canyon "smack-dab" against a big diamond.

*The Fight Continues, Furiously!*

*I Hate You, Mr. Jelly Bean!*

Mr. Jelly Bean then commanded, "Get up, you space scum. I see your rocket ship over there; and I'm giving you just two minutes to get in it and blast off."

*The Loser! The Beat-Up Old Mr. Has Bean*

When ................ saw that Mr. Has Bean was thoroughly beaten in the fight, she/he ran over to Mr. Jelly Bean, and started to shout, "You can't have the gold and diamonds,... you, you, you greedy-guts!"

Well, let me tell you, that beat up old Mr. Has Bean with his broken down antennae barely made it to his rocket ship!

As Mr. Jelly Bean watched him leave, he didn't say a word, but stood firmly with his feet slightly apart and his arms tightly folded over his chest. After Mr. Has Bean's rocket ship lifted off and sped away, Mr. Jelly Bean's antennae slowly stopped sparking and waving around.

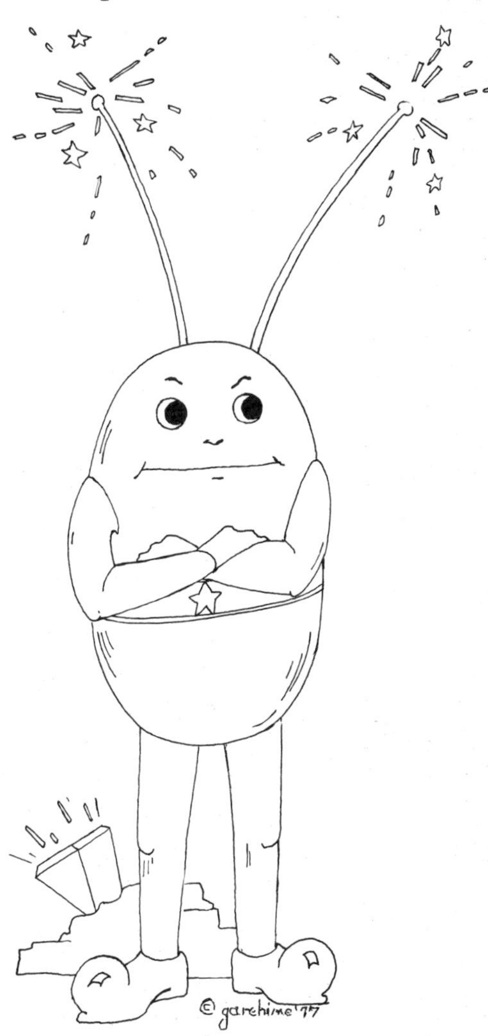


*The Winner!*
*Mr. Jelly Bean*

*The Galactic Space Patrol Will Capture The Bad Mr. Has Bean!*

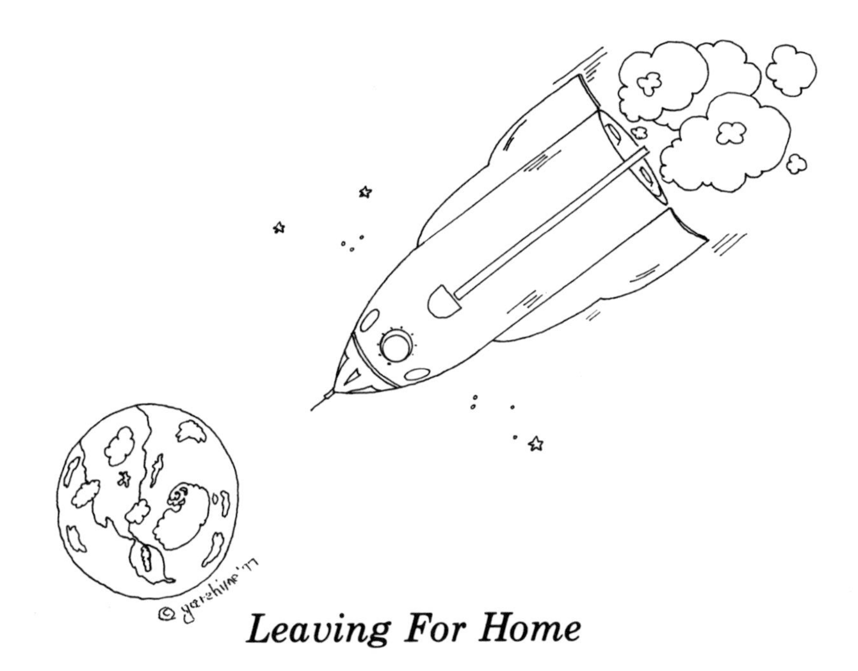

## *Leaving For Home*

Mr. Jelly Bean then turned to ................ and slowly said, "That takes care of him."

"But, Mr. Jelly Bean," ................questioned, "aren't you letting him get away with some gold and diamonds?"

"Oh, he has some gold and diamonds aboard his rocket ship, all right; but he won't get very far, because with my antennae I've already contacted the Galactic Space Patrol. Two of their ships are closing in on him now."

Mr. Jelly Bean paused for a few moments and then said, "Well, ..............., we are going to have to head back to earth if you want to be home in time for your evening meal."

"Oh, Golly!" ................. replied, "I wished that we could explore more of the canyon, but.....could we come back sometime?"

Mr. Jelly Bean said that there was much to see and do on the moon and that they would return as many times as they possibly could.

It didn't take long for them to fly back to the rocket ship and blast off for the trip home. After the controls were set for automatic flight, they had time to relax, to talk, and to discuss plans for future trips.

................. thanked Mr. Jelly Bean for such a wonderful, exciting trip to the moon and for fighting off the bad Mr. Has Bean.

*It Is Lots Of Fun To Fly The Rocket Ship*

*We Have Returned To Earth Again*

Mr. Jelly Bean told ................ that he would like to meet her/his folks sometime, so that they would know that he was honestly and truly a real person. Maybe then they could take a long trip, perhaps to his home planet, Therma.

On the trip back to earth, Mr. Jelly Bean not only let ................ do all of the flying, but he also let her/him bring the rocket ship in for a safe landing close to her/his home.

After they left the ship and were standing by the front door of ................'s home, Mr. Jelly Bean changed ................. back to her/his normal size again.

................. didn't want Mr. Jelly Bean to leave, but Mr. Jelly Bean said that he had to return to Therma for a few weeks and would be back before very long.

After saying their good-byes, ................. watched Mr. Jelly Bean return to his rocket ship, lift off, and quickly disappear into the blue sky.

That evening at the dinner table ................. told her/his folks about the wonderful Mr. Jelly Bean and their trip to the moon. She/He also told them about the gold and diamond canyon and the big fight with Mr. Has Bean. As before, Daddy and Mother winked at each other; not believing what we know to be true, that there really is a Mr. Jelly Bean!

*Good-Bye Mr. Jelly Bean! Come Back Soon!*

*Connect the dots consecutively, then please color me.*